MW00887091

# Yes, Yes, Yaul!

by Jef Czekaj

DISNEY • HYPERION BOOKS

NEW YORK

All rights reserved. Published by Disney • Hyperion Books, an imprint of Disney Book Group. No part of this book may be reproduced or transmitted in any form or by any means, electronic or mechanical, including photocopying, recording, or by any information storage and retrieval system, without written permission from the publisher. For information address Disney • Hyperion Books, 114 Fifth Avenue, New York, New York, 10011-5690.

Printed in Singapore • First Edition • 1 3 5 7 9 10 8 6 4 2 • F850-6835-5-12015

Library of Congress Cataloging-in-Publication Data

Czekaj, Jef.
    Yes, yes, Yaul! / by Jef Czekaj.—1st ed.
        p.  cm.
    Summary: Rap duo Hip the turtle and Hop the rabbit try to convince a prickly porcupine that saying "no" to everything is no fun at all.
    ISBN 978-1-4231-4682-7
    [1. Stories in rhyme. 2. Rap (Music)—Fiction. 3. Porcupines—Fiction. 4. Animals—Fiction. 5. Conduct of life—Fiction.]  I. Title.
    PZ7.C9987Ye 2012
    [E]—dc23            2011026403

Text is set in 22-point Adobe Jenson. Art is created with brush and ink on bristol; color is added using Adobe Photoshop on a Mac.
Reinforced binding • Visit www.disneyhyperionbooks.com

# How to Read This Book!

Whenever you see this rabbit rapping and the words are green, read as fast fast fast as you can.

If this turtle is rapping and you see red words, read as s l o o o o o o o o o w l y as you can.

SOUNDS BORING.

HIP the turtle and HOP the rabbit were best friends and the best rappers in Oldskool County.

It was summertime, so they decided to take their show on the road.

on Turntable Mountain,

and in Lake Boogaloo.

And everywhere they went, animals loved their music.
That is, until the day they played in Sugar Hill Park. . . .

Everybody was having a dope time dancing to the music.

Well, *almost* everybody. One prickly porcupine was not enjoying himself.

After the show, Hip and Hop talked to the mysterious stranger.

Hip and Hop decided to throw Yaul the best surprise birthday party Oldskool County had ever seen.

They smashed a piñata.

They devoured a birthday cake.

And, of course, up-and-coming rap acts threw down some songs.

Some animals said it was the best party Oldskool County had ever seen. But the guest of honor was not impressed.

Luckily, his friends and family had one more trick up their sleeves.

Yaul's aunt had made a special gift for him: a handmade sweater.

It was a little small,

and A LOT itchy.

He had to get it off as soon as possible.

As Yaul scratched and squirmed in his itchy wool sweater, Hip and Hop rapped.

Go, Yaul, go.
Do your dance.
It looks like ants
are in your pants.

Watch his jumps,
and watch his spins.
All you fresh fish,
throw up your fins!

Finally, he got the sweater off.

And so, for the first time ever, he gave a different answer.

It turns out that saying yes was much more fun.

You can probably guess what he said.

The answer was, most definitely, YES!